SHAPES AROUND ME

Rectangles

Anita Loughrey

What is a rectangle?

This is a rectangle. A rectangle has two long sides and two short sides.

Follow your finger around

the edge of the rectangle.

2

Which child is holding the rectangle balloon?

Sue

Zak

Dan

Clare

3

Counting rectangles

Point to the rectangles in the picture.

How many rectangle windows
does the train have?

Answer: 3 rectangles

How many rectangle windows does the railway station have?

Look out of the window. Can you see any rectangle shapes?

Answer: 4 rectangles

Big and small

Rectangles can be different sizes.

big

bigger

small

smaller

biggest

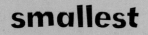

smallest

Coloured rectangles

Rectangles can be different colours.

How many blue rectangles can you see?

How many green rectangles can you see?

8

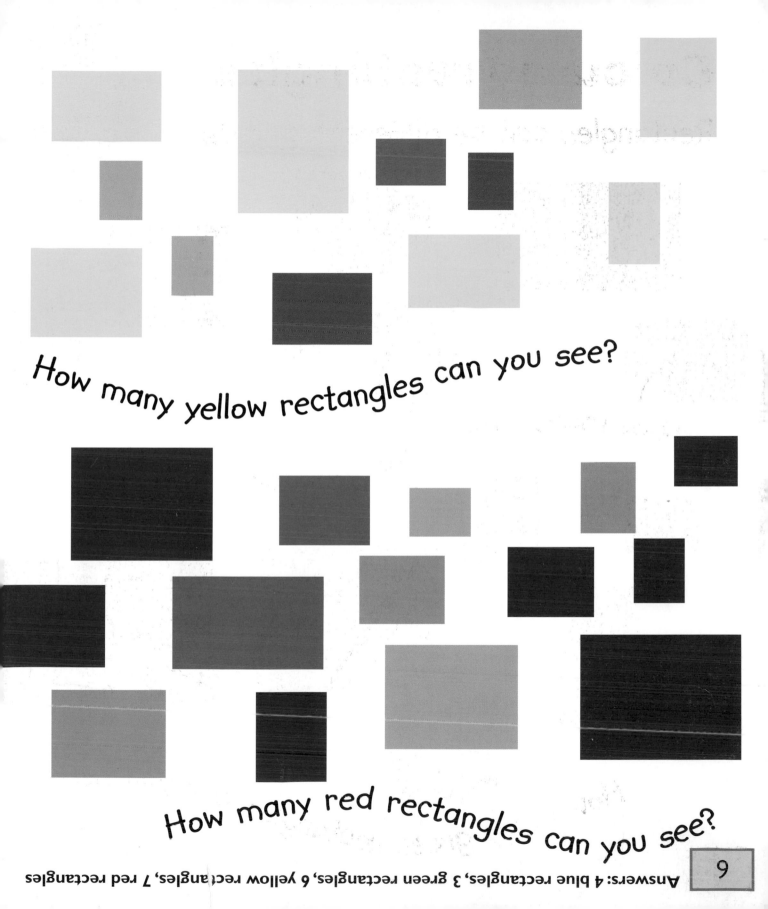

How many yellow rectangles can you see?

How many red rectangles can you see?

Answers: 4 blue rectangles, 3 green rectangles, 6 yellow rectangles, 7 red rectangles

9

Zoom down the track!

Help the tractor follow the path to get to the barn.

How many rectangles does the tractor pass?

Drawing rectangles

Ask an adult to help you
to draw this lorry.

Ask an adult to help you to draw this robot.

In the bedroom

Point to all the
rectangles in
the picture.
Which rectangles
are small?

toybox

robot

rug

What rectangles can you see in your bedroom?

window

picture

drawers

radio

15

At the building site

Point to all the rectangles in the picture. Which is the biggest rectangle?

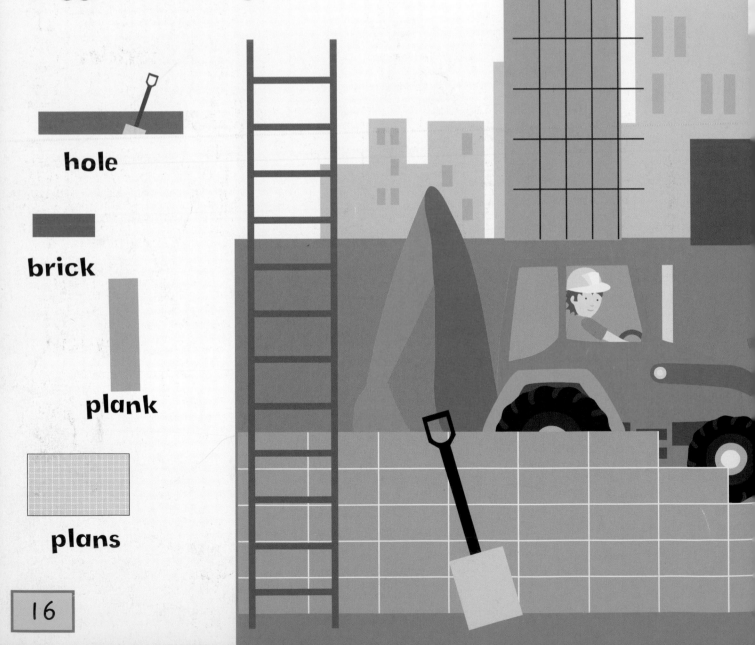

hole

brick

plank

plans

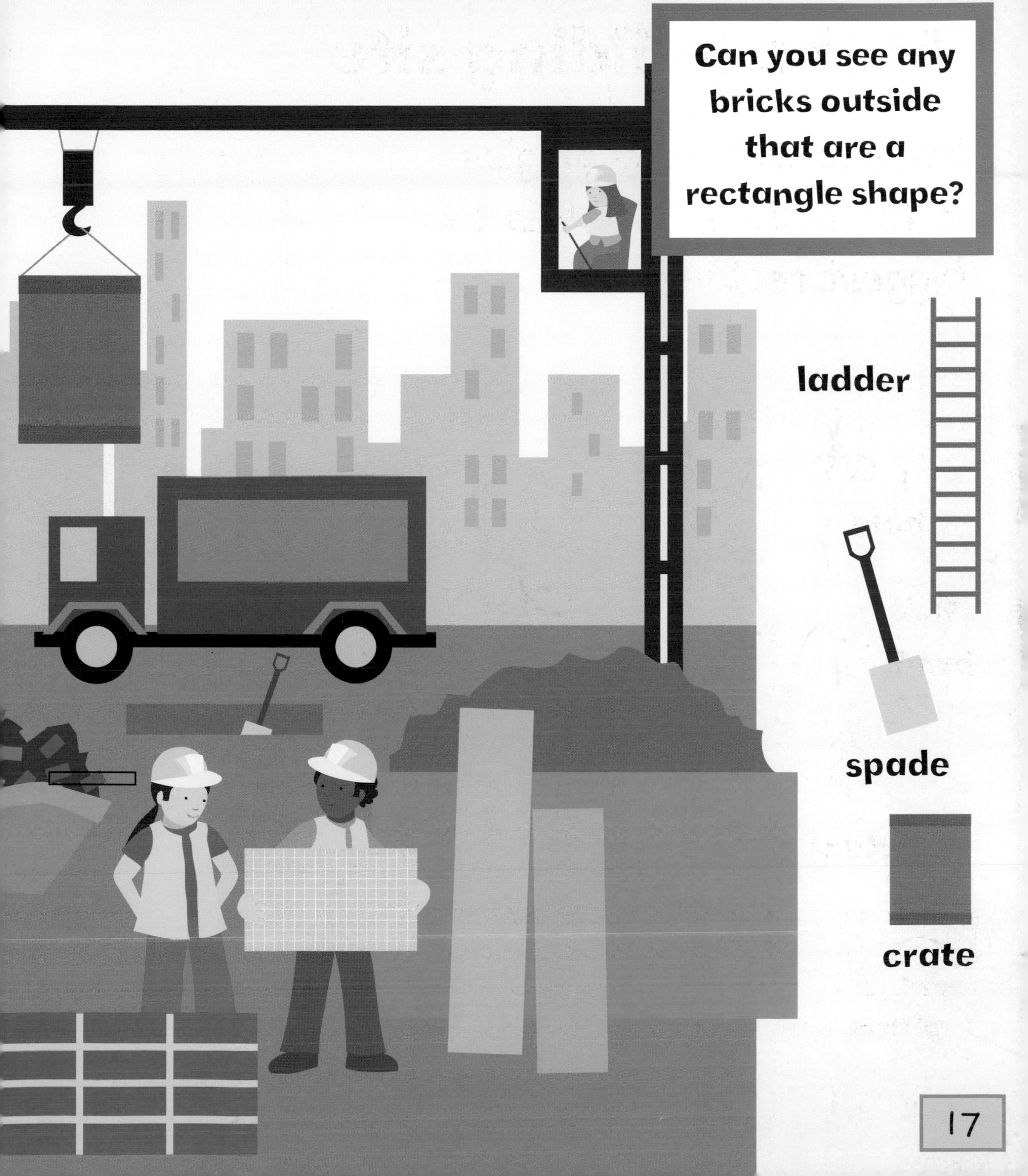

Can you see any bricks outside that are a rectangle shape?

ladder

spade

crate

At the swimming pool

Point to all the rectangles in the picture. Can you spot them all?

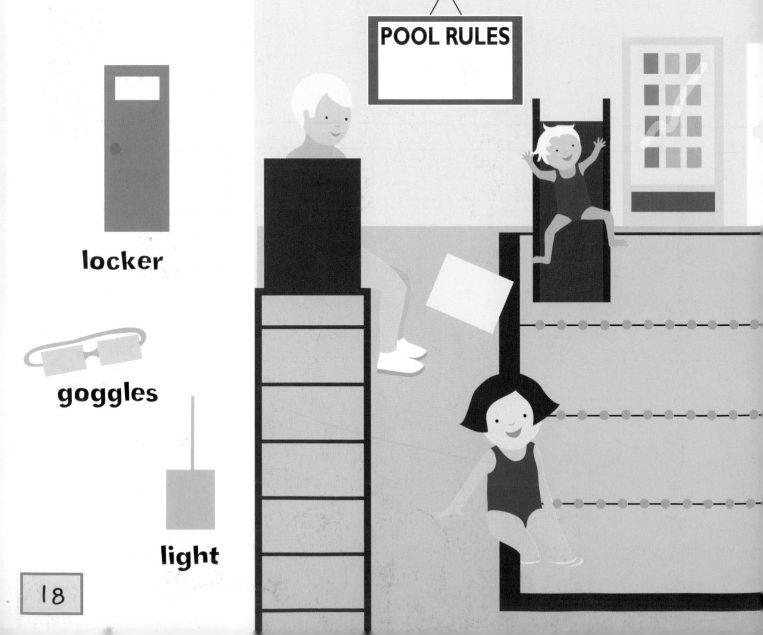

locker

goggles

light

POOL RULES

Have you been to a swimming pool? Did you see these rectangles?

slide

notice board

float

door

In the park

Point to all the rectangles in the picture. Which rectangle is the smallest?

seesaw

climbing frame

slide

Have you been to a park? What rectangles did you see?

flag

drink carton

litter bin

gate

21

At the library

Point to all the rectangles in the picture. Can you name them?

computer

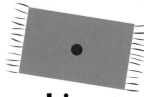

cushion

mouse

Can you find a
rectangle book
at home?

table

book

keyboard

poster

Notes for parents and teachers

This book has been designed to help your child recognize rectangles and to distinguish them from other shapes. The emphasis is on making learning fun, so the book uses the environment to reinforce what your child has seen in the book. The activities help your child to understand the idea of a rectangle shape by using familiar, everyday objects.

Sit with your child and read each page to them. Allow time for your child to think about the activity. Encourage them to talk about what they see. Praise your child when they recognize the items shown in the book from their own experience. If any of the items are unfamiliar to your child, talk about them and explain what they are and where they might be found. Whenever possible, provide opportunities for your child to see the items in the everyday world around them.

Other activities for you to try with your child are:

✹ Play games such as, 'I spy with my little eye something rectangle shaped that begins with...'.

✹ Cut out pictures of different-shaped objects from a catalogue and ask your child to sort them by shape, or to match them to pictures in this book.

✹ Encourage your child to look for things that are rectangle shaped when you are out and about, or play this game at home.

✹ Let your child make collages or junk-models of different rectangle objects, or mould them in clay, so that they can explore the shape by touch.

Remember to keep it fun. Stop before your child gets tired or loses interest and try again another day. Children learn best when they are relaxed and enjoying themselves. It is best to help them to experience new concepts in small steps, rather than to do too much . at once.

Illustrator: Sue Hendra
Editor: Amanda Askew
Designer: Susi Martin

Educational consultant:
Jillian Harker

Copyright © QED Publishing 2010

First published in the UK in 2010 by
QED Publishing
A Quarto Group company
226 City Road
London EC1V 2TT

www.qed-publishing.co.uk

ISBN 978 1 84835 475 3

Printed in China